"COOKIE" A WOUNDED HEALER

"COOKIE"

A WOUNDED HEALER

THERE'S PURPOSE IN PAIN

A.J. HATCHER

XULON PRESS ELITE

Xulon Press Elite
2301 Lucien Way #415
Maitland, FL 32751
407.339.4217
www.xulonpress.com

E^{xulon}LITE

© 2018 by A.J. HATCHER

All rights reserved solely by the author. The author guarantees all contents are original and do not infringe upon the legal rights of any other person or work. No part of this book may be reproduced, stored in a retrieval system, or transmitted in any form or by any means without expressed written permission of the author. The views expressed in this book are not necessarily those of the publisher.

Scripture quotations taken from the King James Version (KJV) – *public domain.*

Printed in the United States of America.

Edited by Xulon Press.

ISBN-13: 9781545652879

Contents

Author's Preface xiii
Introduction xv

Section One: An Illegal Allegiance 1
Chapter One: I Love the New York Life 3
Chapter Two: Welcome to Washington, DC 7
Chapter Three: An Introduction to a Name 9
Chapter Four: She Dropped the Bomb on Me 12
Chapter Five: There's No Place Like Home 18

Section Two: Tragedies into Testimonies 21
Chapter Six: Hello, Michigan, Here We Are 23
Chapter Seven: Home Alone 27
Chapter Eight: Meet and Greet with Death and
　　Disappointment 30
Chapter Nine: Let's Go Home 33
Chapter Ten: The Good, the Bad, and
　　the Very Ugly 38

Section Three: He's There All the Time 43
Chapter Eleven: A Fun Day at the Beach 45
Chapter Twelve: Fish Not Biting 47
Chapter Thirteen: Drinking and Driving
　　Don't Mix 52

"COOKIE" A WOUNDED HEALER

Chapter Fourteen: An Unattended Child Is
    a No-No 55
Chapter Fifteen: Look Both Ways 58
Chapter Sixteen: House of Pestilence 62

Section Four: Year of Demarcation. 65
Chapter Seventeen: An Uninvited Guest 67
Chapter Eighteen: An Appointment to Keep 72
Chapter Nineteen: Run, Cookie, Run 77

Epilogue 85
About the Author. 87

DEDICATION AND ACKNOWLEDGMENT

I want to acknowledge some real life-savers those being a tremendous blessing in my life.

To my father in the Gospel of Jesus Christ, Apostle Ralph E. Green of Free Gospel Deliverance Temple Worldwide: *You* are the one the Lord used to introduce me to Christ and birth me into the Family of God. Thank you for helping me to understand I possess power over all the power of the enemy and the Holy Spirit is a must for making heaven my eternal home. Love you, Sir.

Pastor Dan Johnson, Lifeline Prayer Group in Chicago, Illinois: *Man of God*, you thought enough of me to pray for the masses even when my heart was aching.

Prophetess Ruenette Frasier: Thank *you* for not allowing me to give up on myself through a devastating divorce. Thank you for being my friend who helped me to breathe again.

"COOKIE" A WOUNDED HEALER

Bishop Glen A. Staples of Temple of Praise International Ministries: *Bishop, You are one of a kind*, a unique anointing. You provoke a people to realize what you understand—hope. The anointing on your life instills hope in people. You show the world good things can come out of the 'hood" and education is a key to success.

Bishop Senyo Bulla of Apostolic Breakthrough International Ministries: *Apostolic Man of God* in this end time, you made me understand the Word of God in ways I never imagined; you became my oxygen, a true intercessor, and the reason I gained renewed strength.

Bishop James & Lady Mc Cargo: City of Hope International Ministries: Thank *You Both* for allowing your home to be my family's place of refuge. The City of Hope is truly a home to worship a meeting place where God dwells.

Apostle David Philemon of Church on Fire International Ministries in Cicero, Illinois: *Apostle Philemon* the only man I *know* who builds a people for God 24/7. You live what you preach and what you preach provokes the masses to become better from the inside out. Every day I keep heaven in my view because of you. Apostle (Papa) you're alright with me, and I thank you for interceding for North and South America. You keep on keepin' God famous!

Action Chapel Virginia Bishop Kibby Otto & Pastor Seth there's only two words I can use to show my appreciation from now into eternity, "Thank You".

DEDICATION AND ACKNOWLEDGMENT

This book is dedicated to my family. I hope reading Cookie's story helps you understand life is a conduit that brings tests, trials, and hardships. Although they may seem insurmountable, God uses it all to bring the highest glory. God can and will heal all wounds, and there *is purpose* in pain. I love you all for real, and— trust God—life for you gets better.

PREFACE

*M*y purpose in writing these fictional short story series is to demonstrate through a little girl's trials and tests how life matters and pain has a purpose. How does one live to live? The answer: allow your life to be like a ship.

Apostle David Philemon shares his motto, I've adopted: Life is like a ship, and it can sail millions of miles without sinking, as long as water doesn't get into it. Should water get into the boat, it will begin to sink. So I say to you, allow the Lord to be at the helm of your heart. Don't allow the waters of resentment, bitterness, anger, unforgiveness, and the like to enter into your heart; if you do, your boat will sink. So allow Cookie to be a living didactical presentation of a water bucket to assist in bailing past hurts and adversities out of the boat of your hearts.

INTRODUCTION

*S*he ran when no one chased her, for what is without, only to return to what is within.

Where does she get the power to make you laugh when she's crying inside?

How is she able to lay her hand so gingerly on a shoulder and use the power to comfort when she's discomforted?

How does she command a room and brighten it with her presence when darkness wants to dim the light of her innermost being?

How is she able to speak life and life revives when death is chasing her?

How is she able to heal when she is wounded?

The power she possesses comes from her pain. Some may believe a wounded person is incapable of healing others.

God, the Creator of the Universe, allowed Isaiah the Prophet to prophesy concerning forty and two generations ahead of his day. He records what his eyes saw and his ears heard, "He was wounded for our transgression and bruised for our iniquities. The chastisement of our peace was upon Him and by His stripes, we are healed"

"COOKIE" A WOUNDED HEALER

(Isaiah 53:5). Let us begin this journey. Let us watch this living epistle brings this Scripture to life before our eyes. She will show us how heaven interceded on behalf of a little girl, called Cookie.

SECTION ONE:

An Illegal Allegiance

Chapter One

I Love the New York Life

  *I*n a smoky, dimly lit nightclub, loud music played and every thump of the bass could be felt throughout one's entire being. The clinging of the glasses and the smell of alcohol lingered through the air. The atmosphere of the nightclub electrified with the excitement of laughter. People danced to the beat of the music. Two female strangers danced their way into the women's restroom, laughing. While they both stood at the mirror to freshen their makeup, still laughing, "I'm sorry my name is Lia and yours?" "My name is Juanita." As they parted ways from the restroom the two of them met again and this time it at the bar. Lia asked the bartender, "Mr. Bartender, I'd like a shot of vodka, a glass of water with lemon. Juanita said to the bartender, "Yeah, me too. I'd like a glass of water with lemon, no vodka!." They both burst into laughter. "Wow, it such a pleasure to meet you do you live here in New York? No, I'm from Washington, DC my friends and I come to the City often to party. "Girl, if my husband was home, no way he'd allow me to do this. Oh well, what he doesn't know won't hurt huh? Although

"COOKIE" A WOUNDED HEALER

I can do pretty much as I please. Sometimes I want him home, Lia said." "That's where I differ, says Juanita, I'm not ready for my husband to come home now at all". Her facial expression changed. You're married? Lia asked. Juanita sighs again and says, without immediately answering Lia's question. Juanita responds by saying, "So where's your husband Lia? Oh, he's in the service. "What a coincidence", says, Juanita, "mine is too". Their conversation progressed, they found how much more in common they had.

"So where's yours stationed? Vietnam?"

"Yes, Vietnam."

"Really? Mine too."

I'm sorry, I don't mean to pry, and did I hear you say you don't want your husband to come home? Juanita responded, "well, no and yes, I don't want him to come home too soon.

They continued to pour out the deepest details of their hearts, their two hearts of pain collided. One woman had a lot of guilt and shame while the other filled with emptiness and despair. However, a solution for both is about to be discovered. Juanita began to cry.

"Why are you crying?" Lia asked.

"I'm pregnant."

"Great news, but why are you so sad?"

She paused and sighed. "It's not my husband's baby. How could I be so stupid? I don't want this child. I don't want any man's baby that's not my husband and I don't know what to do." Juanita says.

Lia got up from the barstool and walked over to the musicians and announced. "Hey guys, tell the people to get up. Let's everybody dance! Come on guys, it's a party time. Mr. Bartender, pour everyone a shot. It's on me!" Nothing or no one intimidated her; she acted like she had the answers to everything. Lia danced her way back to the bar stool where Juanita sat while popping her fingers to the music.

"Juanita, may I tell you my deepest desire?"

Juanita said, "Yes, go on."

"I want children, but I am unable to get pregnant."

Juanita sighed and said, "I am pregnant, this is not my husband's child, here you are, wanting a baby, now I'm having a baby I don't want."

"Juanita give me the baby once it's delivered," and Juanita agreed.

"Juanita, okay, here's the plan. Once you go into labor, you assume my identity. Here's my identification card just say your name is Lia, okay? Juanita agreed by saying, "sure." Once you do, the birth certificate will document my name instead of yours."

Juanita, said, "sounds like a plan and she thought, *at least my marriage will be intact and he will never know how unfaithful I've been*. Lia and Juanita embraced.

Lia said, "Okay, see! Problem solved. Don't be sad any longer; we both get what we want."

Lia had a zest for life and a daring personality people couldn't resist. Her friends loved and feared her at the same time. So whatever she wanted to do, her friends would agree, even if she were wrong. Juanita too is mesmerized with Lia.

No one could match wits with Lia. She could've been in the halls of justice because of her crafty ability to persuade. Lia's a well-educated woman. She received two master degrees, one in childhood education and the other in business. She went further to receive her doctorate in psychology. Her persona presented her in such

"COOKIE" A WOUNDED HEALER

a way as though she ruled the universe she likened herself to God the Creator. After the encounter with Juanita, early the next morning Lia and her friends returned home to Washington, DC.

CHAPTER TWO

Welcome to Washington, DC

    Several months went by, Juanita hadn't called. Lia said aloud to herself, "Perhaps it's a dream; either way, did that conversation really happen? Did I meet Juanita?" She shrugged it off.

    Lia tried to rid the thoughts of having a child; however, she continued to ponder about it. Not many days thereafter, the doorbell rang, and as she got closer to the door, she saw what looked like a baby blanket in the arms of a woman. She opened the door, and to her surprise, there stood Juanita, with tears in her eyes.

    Juanita began to tell the story about the birth of the baby. "The birth pain was so unbearable, I forgot the plan, your identification card, and you! Once I had her, I gave her to an old woman in Harlem. I felt something had to be wrong and my suspicion was right. The old woman wasn't caring for her properly. Look at her! She's severely underweight, isn't she! She can barely hold her little head up and her little body is so limp. She's nine months old shouldn't she be moving more than this! Lia, I remembered the conversation I had with you. I can't keep her! I really can't! My husband

"COOKIE" A WOUNDED HEALER

will kill me if he ever finds this out, but I don't want this baby to die! Please! Lia, please, will you take her, please?" Lia extended her arms to take the baby.

Juanita's hand-delivered the baby into Lia'a waiting arms. Lia stood motionless looking at the young mother and the child. *I must be dreaming*, she thought. *This is no dream, this is real."* Lia's heart filled with love as she realized a dream come true.

Juanita placed the baby in Lia's arms. She turned to walk away, stopped, and turned back to Lia and said, "You wanted a baby, so here she is, and by the way, name her, please. I don't want to know."

"Juanita, wait! Before you go, where are her clothes and birth certificate?" Lia asked.

"I don't have anything for her."

Hurriedly she rushed into a waiting cab, never to be heard from again.

Lia, a new mother, something she dreamed of becoming. There's nothing she wanted outside of her reach more than being able to birth her own child. Now Lia's even more untouchable and courageous like Queen Jezebel; now, this "Queen" had a child.

Chapter Three

An Introduction to a Name

*L*ia a new mother, she's so excited like a child with a brand new toy. She's overwhelmed with the thought of motherhood. However, she didn't weigh the cost, whether any consequences would occur by taking this child. Juanita's gone, now Lia's thinking, *will the police come for me? Will they think I stole this baby? What will my parents think? What will my husband think? What if she gets sick and I need Juanita? How am I going to contact her? What's Juanita's last name? Oh my God, where does she live? Well, whatever who cares about consequence! I'm not going to worry about it! My name is Lia! I can handle this!*

She wrapped the baby back into the tethered blanket and rushed to her parents' home. Lia burst through the door, a bundle of joy in her arms. Her entire being illuminated with enthusiasm and joy. She couldn't stop giggling.

"I got a baby, and it's a girl!" she said.

Lia's father said, "You? What? Where did you get this thing from?"

"COOKIE" A WOUNDED HEALER

Lia's mother gently rebuked her husband. Lia told her parents how she got the baby. " my friends and I went to New York to hang out. I met this poor girl who cheated on her husband, she wanted me to care for the child." Lia left out some details of her story. Her father didn't buy her explanation. He stares at the baby and could tell the baby needed medical attention.

He told Lia, "Return the baby to its mother at once. You cannot always have your way. I'm so sorry. I've made a grave mistake in allowing you everything you wanted as a child. Lia, I told your mother many times stop allowing you your way about everything. This is wrong; take the child back at once! Daughter, you can go to jail! Look at this baby she's sick! What will your husband think? What in the world has gotten into you? Did you consider this is a bad idea?" "Daddy, I always wanted a baby, the baby's mother doesn't want her, she cannot keep her cause, huh, well, this baby is not her husband's child. If he finds out he will divorce her. Oh daddy, it's' going to be alright I can handle it".

Lia's mother, on the other hand, took the child in her arms and fell in love with the baby at first sight. This new grandmother said to her husband, "Watch your words because this child may be the one who gives you a drink of water one day. Don't speak mean words over her it's not her fault she didn't ask to come here!"

"What's her name?" asked Lia's mom.

"I guess she doesn't ?"Said Lia.

"No, honest, what's her name?" demanded her parents while they both stared at Lia waiting for an answer.

The conversation between Lia and her parents lasted for most of the afternoon. Lia rehashed the same story over and over until her dad threw his hands in the air

AN INTRODUCTION TO A NAME

in disgust and said, "Who cares about a name—where did this baby come from? I'm not your mother and I am not buying your explanation, period!" He turned and walked away not wanting nothing more to do with this notion.

At this point, the newly pronounced grandmother wasn't concerned about who, what, or when. She said, "Let me look at her again. I know what I'm gonna call her! We will call her 'Cookie' because she looks like a cookie."

Okay," said Lia, "Cookie it is."

Lia's about to embark on the real work of motherhood. Her mind, as brilliant as it is, started to ponder. *Has the baby had any medical care? She needs baby clothes. Does she eat table food? What kind of milk does she drink? What will happen if she starts to cry? What will I do?* The reality of it all became overwhelming. Lia never cared for a baby before. She had to consult her mother for advice.

Chapter Four

She Dropped the Bomb on Me

W hile the United States was engaged in the Vietnam War, a child named Cookie' born and both situations were equally confusing: the war and the baby. Somewhere in South Vietnam, a call came from the United States, "Sergeant, the telephone is for you".

An excited voice on the other end said, "It's a girl! What shall we name her?"

"Hello," he said. "Lia, is this you?"

"Sweetheart, it's me. We got a baby girl."

The man on the other end of the telephone line is, Lia's husband. He's one of the most courageous decorated Sergeants in the US Armed Forces. This being his third tour of duty. The Vietnam War is the bloodiest he fought in. Nothing he encountered in all the three wars prepared him for the war he would face in his marriage when he returned home.

While fighting for his country, thousands of miles away, he began pondering in his mind, *a child. But wait, how can this be? I'm here in South Vietnam while my wife is at home in Washington, DC. It doesn't add up ... this must've happened while home on furlough,*

SHE DROPPED THE BOMB ON ME

but wait! I was in Panama in September. This happened before I left the States? Perhaps when we were in Washington State? No time to think about a baby. Stay focused. He shook the thoughts and regained himself only to ponder on this issue again. *I'm responsible for the lives of my soldiers and to defend my Country. Could it be ... maybe ... my wife had an affair? Wait! Get yourself together and focus!*

Last he knew they couldn't conceive children. No time to keep pondering over the thoughts racing through his mind. While holding a telephone to his ear, he named the baby, giving her a formal name and hangs up the telephone. *Did she say....if...she had a baby what would I name her? She's off on a tangent I will get to the bottom of this when I get back to the States.*

Sergeant received a two-page letter from his wife. He read the letter in haste as he tried to get through the mutter for an explanation of *how* his wife had a baby. At the bottom of the second page is a request for his signature. A blank document with the instructions: "Fill in the blanks below. Write legibly baby given name, mother's name, and father's name and please sign below."

Overhead air raids, sirens, and as banana boats flew, so he tucked the papers away. On a rare day of calm, he took the crumpled letter out of his bag in a hope to understand what kind of request is this. Is this an adoption request or a birth certificate request? He's more bewildered than before. The last letter she had written him expressed how lonely and worried hearing the news reports about the war.

"I haven't fathered any children, and the baby's born in January? I'm in another country. It can't be mine."

"Mail call"! Hey, Sargent here's one for you!"

"COOKIE" A WOUNDED HEALER

However reluctant he opened the letter, and it read:

Dear honey, Thank you for naming our daughter. She is so beautiful. Here's her picture. We cannot wait for you to come home. Love you and P.S., I took her to the military hospital for a check-up and she has her shots. Love forever, Lia.

He's dumbfounded thinking, *how could she do this?* He remembered the request to legalize the child, but he still had the papers with him. She forged his name and signature. Months went by before he's able to return home. Thoughts of the possibilities of his wife's infidelities still lingered in his mind. Finally, he arrived back home a decorated war hero. He wore medals across the shoulders and breast of his uniform jacket. What a sight to behold he's awarded the National Defense Service Medal with Leaf Cluster, Vietnam Services Medal with two Bronze Service Stars, Republic of Vietnam Campaign Medal with Device 1960, Bronze Star Medal, Republic of Vietnam Cross of Gallantry with Bronze Star, Good Conduct Medal (fourth award), and two Overseas Service Bars. There he stood at the door of the house all gallant without saying a word. His appearance spoke announced him.

Someone hollered, "Hey Lia, guess who's here?"

"Who?"

"Your husband; he's here at the door!"

As he came through the door, he stopped in his tracks; there stood the baby girl who bore his name. She's beautiful her hair was silky black and curly. She had the biggest and brightest brown eyes. It's hard to

SHE DROPPED THE BOMB ON ME

stop looking and wondering about her. He canvased the room and noticed people everywhere, the stench of alcohol and tobacco permanent the air. The little girl turned and ran back through the crowd of people as if she mysteriously disappeared into a blanket of smoke. It's difficult for him to breathe and focus because of the second-hand smoke as he attempted to locate her again. *Perhaps I can deal with the idea of having a daughter. I've been through a lot, and I've learned to accept a lot; it's not so bad*, he thought. "I can love this beautiful baby girl," he said to himself.

From a distance, a female appeared, not his wife, in front of everyone, in a manner to impress this well-dressed decorated war hero, hey, "little girl, where is your "putty cat"?

"What kind of question to ask of a toddler?" he said aloud. "What is a putty cat?"

The baby placed her hand in front of her diaper in response. Furious at what he saw and heard. He thought without responding, *who are all of these derelicts and drunks in my house, and where is my wife?* He backed himself to the door and reached without looking for his duffle bag to leave.

All of a sudden, Lia appeared, reluctantly and said, "Hi, honey, "Not wanting to see him, having to explain what's going on in his own home. Lia did not expect him, and if she knew he was coming, she'd made certain the house would be cleared. Lia's husband never saw this side of her before. She said to him, "You surprised me. Why you didn't let me know you were coming home. I would've had a homecoming celebration for you." Lia's thinking and talking to her husband at the same time. *Think oh, what to do Jay's in the kitchen,*

"COOKIE" A WOUNDED HEALER

maybe I'll say his ah, plumber, or... "Babe how are you." Lia searches her mind for the right words to say.

He skipped all introductions—no hugging or kissing, void of love pierced through his eyes only anger. He told his wife how disappointed he felt.

"What is going on here? Who are these bums, and what in the world has happened to you? When did you start having liquor in my house? Who is this trifling woman, the one who called out to me? I don't know any of these people and why are these women so disgusting? Who are these men in my house! Oh God, what rock did you find these people under? How dare you? When did you start smoking? Have I been gone that long! This is still my house, Lia! Aside from all this, a child is here! You've turned our home into a gambling den! Have you lost your mind?

He continued to scold her for having a child in an environment like this. "I don't know you, you've changed! You are different from the woman I fell in love with, and one day soon I will return to take the child from you.

His eyes were full of rage, and the veins in his temples pulsated. He was angry. He even forgot to ask her about the forging of his name on the birth certificate. He also forgot to ask how she came about having a baby in the first place. Anger consumed him; he turned and slammed the door so hard behind him, the house shook from its foundation.

The last medal crossed his heart, the medal of betrayal. He shouted toward the closed door, "Lia, I want a divorce!"

Lia didn't tell her husband she had another man in her life and he played the role of a father to Little

SHE DROPPED THE BOMB ON ME

Cookie. He was in the kitchen and overheard their conversation but he did not come out from there. He knew about her husband, but her husband did not know about him. She knew to say nothing about her boyfriend if so, the situation could've been worse.

Chapter Five

There's No Place Like Home

Cookie awoke to the sound of glass breaking from downstairs.

Someone is fighting. I wonder who has the nerve to cross my mother she is a tyrant. Something is wrong, she thought. She got out of the bed and walked softly to the banister and peeked through the railing bars and saw a fight; blood is all over the kitchen. Her mother's hitting her daddy with a bottle, and blood ran down his face. Cookie's watching as he's trying to block the bottle from hitting him anymore.

"Why! Why! No! Mommy, stop it! Stop it!" she screamed at the top of her lungs.

Not long after they fought, daddy left the house. He had put up with a lot of Lia's shenanigans for the sake of the love he had for Lia and the little girl. He's the only father Cookie knew of. He's the man her mother fell in love with while her husband was away in the war.

Lia's attitude didn't change after being confronted by her husband or when her boyfriend left. Friday through early Sunday mornings Lia's house was the place to be. Bookies came to the house five days a

THERE'S NO PLACE LIKE HOME

week and cases of liquor were delivered twice a month. Every weekend Lia made lots of money bootlegging, gambling, and selling fried chicken and fish dinners. Lia's house is no boring place. The only children's book located in the house, Dr. Seuss' *The Cat in the Hat*; however, a lot of adult paperback instruction booklets how to place bets laid on the end tables throughout the house.

Not one of Lia's adult friends brought their children over for the weekend. Lia's environment, absolutely no good for children. Some of Lia's friend's amused themselves by giving Cookie alcohol and watched as the intoxicated toddler fell over herself as though it were funny. What conscious individual would allow a child to sip liquor out of a glass and watch the child staggered about and fall?

Someone had left a glass of liquor in the upstairs bathroom, and Cookie drank all of it. The room began to spin as she tried to walk. She tumbled down a flight of stairs—sixteen stairs in total. She landed at the bottom of the staircase, waiting for her mother or someone to pick her up from the floor. She was unable to gain any control over herself. The smoke from cigarettes was so thick, you could almost part the smoke with a pair of hands. *It's difficult to breathe. Is someone coming to help me get up from here?* she thought. Cookie had difficulty trying to see with her little bloodshot eyes. She began to think, w*ill anyone at least open a window?* No one thought it necessary to open a window or to stop smoking long enough to allow the child or themselves to breathe fresh air. The only way for her to breathe was to pant like a dog.

"COOKIE" A WOUNDED HEALER

Finally, Lia came. "Cookie, get up from there! What happened to you?" Lia saw how difficult it was for Cookie to get up from the floor, so she helped her up and carried her to her bedroom and placed her on her bed, not questioning what happened to her. So much recklessness, drama, illegal selling of alcohol, gambling, and numbers running at their house. The only comfort Cookie had from all of the madness was time spent at her grandparents.

SECTION TWO:

Tragedies into Testimonies

CHAPTER SIX

Hello, Michigan, Here We Are

*L*ia called her mom and said, "Mom, I'm moving to Michigan".
"What's the reason for uprooting so sudden? Your father and I don't think this is a wise decision. Lia, what have you done? Are you in trouble?" No mom I need a change. Jay and I are broken up and beside Michigan will be good for Cookie. Mom, you still there? I brought a house. I gave Boyce money to purchase it. Mom, hello are you listening to me?" "Yes, Lia, I'm listening, says her mother. Lia sweetheart let Cookie stay here with us. She can go to school here. Your father and I will take care of her while you go and get yourself together, ok?" "Mom, I love you and dad but this is what I want to do she's going with me! I will call you back later." Lia's mother sighs and hangs the phone up. Grandma's not too keen concerning this abrupt notice of their leaving. The telephone rang again, "Hello, mom it's me again. Mom, there's a teaching opportunity in Michigan, and besides I need a change of scenery please understand."

Lia was unsuccessful in trying to convince her mother of the great teaching opportunity. Grandma

"COOKIE" A WOUNDED HEALER

began to talk to someone else not paying Lia any attention; although Lia is talking, grandma is ignoring her, moving the telephone from her ear. *Lord! Lord, please take care of my daughter and granddaughter, Lia is troubled about something. Lord, I am worried I feel like there's more to the story. Why the need to leave in such a rush? It's all too familiar. This wasn't the first time—she left in a hurry before; to, Philadelphia, South Carolina, New York, and now, Michigan!*

Grandma phoned Lia's ex-boyfriend Jay the only man Cookie knew as dad. Although grandma worried about Lia she's more so worried about Little Cookie.

"Hello, Mr. Jay, this is Lia's mother. I'm worried about her; she's decided to move to Michigan and take my Little Cookie. I know you love them. Lia is so irresponsible; I'm so afraid of what may happen to them. If you can, will you make sure she's is okay? Maybe you can talk her out of it? I'm worried to death!"

"Ma'am, I promised I will make sure she's okay. I didn't know they're leaving, and she knows how much I love Cookie. Ma'am, I love her like she's my own child; don't worry," he said and hung up the telephone. Jay pondered what prompted Lia's sudden reasons for leaving? *Who did she hurt or has someone double-crosses her? Does she owe someone money? I will go and find out what's going on.*

The year is1965 when they moved to Michigan. Lia had purchased a house before leaving Washington, DC. Michigan is so beautiful in the wintertime. The snow as white as cotton and due to the sun's reflection atop the snow, it made the snow to glisten as though the purest crystal covered the earth. It's blinding and breathtaking, all at the same time. To focus without sunglasses is virtually impossible.

The air frigidly cold when they arrived. It was a record snowfall that year. The snowfall created mountains made of snow. Cookie looked and said, "snow is everywhere and the snow clouds cover the ground like a gigantic blanket.

The next morning, when they awoke, more snow had fallen. Neighbors were friendly, showing compassion for one another. Whenever the snowfall is enormous neighbors helped one another barricaded by the snow to get out of their homes.

A few days later, someone knocked on the door. "It's daddy, with a trunk," screams Cookie.

"He's come to live with us and to take care of me, as he promised grandma!" she said to her mother.

Jay kept his word to grandma to follow the heart of the little girl. They hadn't seen each other since that terrible fight. Lia was surprised to see him. Cookie was overjoyed because daddy had come to Michigan. It was not long before Lia's old habits begin to manifest. People came over to gamble all night and she started selling alcohol again.

Jay, of course, did not approve, and he told her how he felt. "This new environment has become the same unhealthy environment you created in Washington, DC, to say the least."

"Lia, why would you come here for a change only to behave the same? It's not safe for you to continue breaking laws; don't think for one minute what you are doing is good for Cookie. She's a little girl. Please allow her to be just that!"

"COOKIE" A WOUNDED HEALER

Lia hated anyone telling her what to do. "Get out! Get out now!" she screamed.

"Daddy, please don't leave me. I don't want you to leave me," said Cookie. She confronted her mother, although terrified. She begged, "Mother! Please don't put my dad out in the cold with nowhere to go! Please."

Grandmother's words resounded in Jay's ears: "Mr. Jay, please take care of my grandbaby". Jay began to ponder in his mind, *what measure of love I have for this child? I've never fathered a child before. I love this child so much so I left his home, my family, my job, and my friends to follow a woman who clearly refuses to respect me. In all efforts to follow the heart of a little girl. I've put up with a lot for the sake of love for this little girl. God, what am I to do?*

He told Cookie, "baby daddy loves you to the bone and I will kill a brick for you. You know I.. baby it will be alright" as he tried to keep back the tears. He left Lia for good. Cookie stood by the open door, watching her daddy as he had a difficult time carrying a trunk through the deep snow. She felt helpless. She didn't feel the cold wind blowing through her pajamas, nor the nose hairs that began to freeze with each breath she took. Her extremities became numb due to the bitter cold. The wind created snowdrifts, which became clouds engulfed and carried her dad away. Tears filled her little eyes as she spoke to the wind and asked, "Why so much pain?"

Chapter Seven

Home Alone

Although the partying continued every weekend, a sudden change occurred after the conversation Jay had with Lia. She stopped the gambling at home every weekend. She alternated the weekends by gambling at someone else house while leaving her baby at home alone. Before she would leave her five-year-old home, she gave her explicit instructions: "Do not open the door for anyone."

Lia's instruction more so to cover her own irresponsibility than of caution?

Mother said, "Cookie, I'm only going across the street to Ms. Thomas' house, so don't open the door for anyone."

Of course, she would not open the door. She's afraid of getting a beating if she did. The gambling parties continued every weekend without interruption. One weekend at home, and the next week the parties at Ms. Thomas' house. One Friday evening Cookie heard, knock! knock! on the door.

Oh no! What do I do? She thought. *I hope they go away. Mommy's not here.* She remembered her mother's instruction not to open the door for anyone. Whoever's knocking at the door is now knocking on the living room windows. She saw a face peering through the window. It's daddy!

"Daddy, mommy said not to open the door."

He began to talk with her through the window. Did you eat, she says, no. Although afraid, aside from her mother's instructions, she opened the door to let him in. He cooked for her, brushed her hair, kissed her, and said, "Talk to you later."

Before he closed the door, he said, "Do not tell your mother."

"Okay, daddy, I promise."

At that point he thought of a secret knock so once she heard the knock; it would be safe to open the door. After her dad visited, she grew more afraid of being left alone in a big house. She asked her mother for a dog or a cat, and her mother bought both. Lia named the dog Duchess and the cat Twinkles. The three of them got along fine. Mother taught Cookie how to make sandwiches when she's alone. Cookie was a good sandwich maker. She made sandwiches for herself, Duchess and Twinkles when they were alone watching television.

Duchess' a black retriever, and Twinkles, large old gray cat, who ruled the house with his snarling and hissing. Mother had an ottoman in the living room, and if one of her friends wanted to sit there, Twinkles would refuse to move. Twinkles and Duchess protected and ruled the house. Although she felt safe and secure with them, she still needed her mother to be home with her.

One weekend more frightening than any other while they were alone. Mr. Jay knocked using their secret knock and got no response. He became worried because

HOME ALONE

Cookie took long to open the door. She was severely ill and couldn't raise her voice above a whisper "daddy." He peered through the living room window and he didn't spot her. He's frantic. He went to the side window, and there he saw his daughter on the floor by the stairs." Cookie, baby get up! Baby, please come open the door!" She's weak but determined to crawl up the stairs to the door. *Daddy the room is spinning I'm trying I'm gonna throw up.* He violently pushes while turning the doorknob, trying to get in as he's pressing his shoulder with all of his strength to break in. She got to the door and mustered enough strength to turn the lock. He rushed in and picked her up from the floor, holding her almost lifeless body in his arms. Something's dreadfully wrong off to the hospital, they went.

Cookie diagnosed with the rare flu called the Hong Kong Flu, and she could have died, had she been left longer. She had laid on the sofa for two days before her dad came by. Perhaps she would have died had it not been for her dad and her friends Duchess and Twinkles, who stayed by her side Twinkles jumped on top of her chest purring while Duchess barked and licked her hand. Cookie's daddy told her mother only after he brought her back home from the hospital.

Chapter Eight

Meet and Greet with Death and Disappointment

One afternoon, Duchess and Cookie went outside to play, Cookie asked Twinkles, "Do you want to come outside to play?"

Twinkle liked taking baths and going outside to play. She asked him the second time, "Do you want to go outside?"

Twinkles looked at her and turned his head in the opposite direction. He ignored her. Although he's only a cat, and of course cats cannot speak, his body language spoke loud and clear. Twinkles is somewhat like Garfield the cat or Oscar the Grouch on Sesame Street. He's very grumpy, but she loved him, and he loved her back.

Before she could finish with Twinkles, they heard the sound of tires squeal and a loud boom, and all of a sudden, Duchess belted out a loud scream at the top of her lungs. She's hit by a car. Duchess' back is broken, but she determined to get to Cookie. She pulled herself by her two front legs from across the street, up to the driveway now to the walkway leading into the house. Poor Duchess, crying and in so much pain as she pulled herself with her front two paws.

Cookie's crying and her mother called the police as Duchess lay at her feet while she stroked Duchess' head. Someone once said never to touch a wounded animal because it may attack in defense. However, it didn't apply to Duchess because she's a wounded healer to heal Cookie's, broken heart. They looked into each other's eyes for the last time to say a final goodbye.

The police officer arrived, and he took out his revolver and shot and killed Duchess to take her out of her misery. After the bang sound of his gun, he gave the little girl the shell casing. Duchess died right in front of her. Cookie started to cry and said in her heart, *a shell casing is a souvenir? I don't want an empty shell? I want Duchess life brought back in my four-legged friend.* "Thank you, Officer, come on Cookie let's go inside," Lia said. Cookie stood with her eyes fixed on Duchess lifeless body waiting and hoping she would suddenly get up. "Come on lets' go, inside". Lia took her by the hand to walk inside the house.

Not long after, Twinkles ran away, never to return. Maybe it's too much for him to endure. Of course, it's too much for her. She'd lost both of her best friends.

Not many days later, Lia called her parents to let them know she would be leaving Michigan soon. Perhaps this is her way of easing the pain Cookie felt.

"Hello dad, I'm thinking it may be best for me and Cookie to come home. She is having a tough time since her dog died and her cat ran away. I drove around looking everywhere for him. I even went to the animal shelter. Dad, I don't know what else to do?" "Okay, child, come on home everything is going to be alright. Lia your mother and I want you to return within the week". "Yeah, dad I'm coming home". Cookie overheard their conversation she's so elated they were going back home to Washington, DC.

Chapter Nine

Let's Go Home

      ack in Washington, DC, things were quiet. Cookie never understood the reason why her mother left so suddenly but she's glad to be home nonetheless. She hoped things would be different after all they had been through in Michigan.

Mr. Jay decided to stay in Michigan because he had a job at the airport. They could travel anywhere in the United States for free, and he made sure of it. She didn't want to leave without her dad; however, the joy of being with her grandparents overruled everything else. Her grandparents were glad their babies were back at home. Grandmother always prayed for them, and she taught Cookie how to pray to God, although they didn't go to church.

Every year, for Easter, grandpa gave grandma money for shopping, and she and Cookie took the trolley downtown to go shopping at Garfunkel's Department Store. It was such a treat for them to go shopping. Grandma would wake Cookie early in the morning to catch the trolley.

"COOKIE" A WOUNDED HEALER

Grandma loved people. As people would pass by, she'd say, "Good morning, sir. Good morning, ma'am. Have a wonderful day." Some would reply, "Same to you." Whenever grandma opened her mouth to speak, she'd speak with a smile. Her smiles were contagious. One could not help but smile in return. Grandma showed so much love by her behavior; her love for humankind resonated from her amidst hatred and bigotry, and yet, grandma's heart remained pure.

Shopping is fun, but grandma would get tired fast. They took a break from shopping, to sit in the park to feed the birds. In fact, she loved birds as much as she loved people. Grandma had birds of her own she raised canaries. She treated her birds like they were children. Every Saturday morning, after she took care of her birds, she made sure she'd go to the park to feed the other birds. It's a Saturday ritual for grandma. While they were feeding the birds, Cookie had many questions for her grandmother. "Grandma," she asked, "what causes some grown-ups to be so cruel and why is there death, why is it? Grandma, please help me to understand."

Oh, how difficult to explain to a child about death and why some people are so cruel, grandmother pondered. She sighed taking a long breath and answered the best she could, simply by saying, "Child, grandma doesn't know."

They continued to throw bird seeds to the ground watching the birds perch to eat. After they finished feeding the birds, they went home. She never wanted to be without her grandparents. There's no greater feeling for a child to love and to be loved in return. .Cookie's grandparents' home is a safe place and especially in

LET'S GO HOME

grandma's bed. Grandma had the highest bed and bed-posts she had ever seen. To sleep in her bed is like floating on a cloud of marshmallows. Every night, grandma brushed Cookie's hair 100 strokes. Right after they got on their knees to pray before going to sleep. As long as she stayed with her grandparents, she had no fears or concerns about all of the turmoil at her mother's house.

Every morning, the smell of fresh bread baking would wake her. The scent of the bread tickled her nose down to her belly. No foul odors or language came from her grandparent's mouths; how peaceful it is at their home. She's a little girl there. Even though, she didn't have any human friends she had friends—friends the naked eye could not envision. They were supernatural, invisible ones as old as life itself. Some of them she named Love, Time, Laughter, Sharing, Courage, and Peace, and all were dear to her. She held onto them so tight, she wouldn't part with them no matter what, and to live without them until today would be unimaginable. She came to know some of them as the Fruits of the Spirit. Those are all a part of her DNA, and the only way to witness them with the naked eye is to experience them. She learned to embrace the characteristics of the Fruit of the Spirit as friends because they will never die nor will they mislead anyone.

Mr. Time the oddest of all. Although he's not a Fruit of the Spirit he's the hardest one to embrace. When it appears he's standing still, Mr. Time is actually moving, and he never appears to stop. He's now, before, and beyond. Mr. Time is like the wind: he comes and goes, yet he is always present. Time is marked by eternity; this is where he comes out of.

35

"COOKIE" A WOUNDED HEALER

One night as she's with her grandparents waiting for the taxicab to take her home, she fell asleep. Mr. Time appeared to her in a dream and said things hard to understand. He said, "The power of the earth is in the hand of the Lord, and in due season, He sets over it one who's profitable, and that one is me-Time. You call me Mr. Time, so let me help you to understand me. I'm marked by seasons, and seasons are appointed occasions."

He went further to say, "To everything, there are a season and a time to every purpose under the heaven: a time to be born and a time to die; a time to plant and a time to pluck up that which was planted; a time to kill and a time to heal; a time to break down and a time to build up; a time to weep and a time to laugh; a time to mourn and a time to dance; a time to cast away stones and a time to gather stones together; a time to embrace and a time to keep from embracing; a time to get and a time to lose; a time to keep and a time to cast away; a time to tear and a time to sow; a time to keep silence and a time to speak; a time to love and a time to hate; and a time to make war and a time of peace. God has made everything beautiful in His time, and it shall be forever; nothing can be put to it nor taken away from it."

Beep! Cookie's awakened by the sound of a car horn. "Child, get up; time to get ready to go home," said grandpa.

Grandpa walked her downstairs. As they got closer to the taxicab, she loosened his hand to hug his neck. Grandpa opened the rear door of the taxi and gave the driver a stern look and told him, "Be careful with my granddaughter and don't drive too fast!"

As grandpa walked away he stopped, turned back with the same stern look and said, "Grandma and I will

LET'S GO HOME

wait by the phone for a call. Make sure your mother calls the minute you get into the house."

"Yes, sir, I will. I love you papa; bye-bye."

Grandpa smiled and closed the cab door. She watched him as he watched with his eyes fixed on the taxi driver as they pulled away.

Chapter Ten

The Good, the Bad, and the Very Ugly

*T*he cab pulled up to the house, Lia thanked the driver for bringing her daughter home safe. As Cookie on her way upstairs to her bedroom, she overheard her mother say, "Pete owes me money, so let's teach him a lesson."

Oh no, not again; we haven't been home two months yet. Perhaps they've forgotten I'm here and can hear them? Cookie thought. She did not want to hear a plan or to witness it unfold. She heard a voice inside saying, "close your door, and pray a little prayer for Uncle Pete." "Lord, please don't let them hurt Mr. Pete he's a nice man, thank You, Lord, Amen". After praying she laid down to go to sleep wanting Saturday morning to hurry. Cookie was looking forward to Saturday because it was the third Saturday of the month.

Every third Saturday, her neighborhood would be awakened by the sounds of music megaphones and bells ringing. Doors and windows opened early because of the parade of merchants who came to the neighborhood

THE GOOD, THE BAD, AND THE VERY UGLY

selling food and other items. Some came on wagons and horses, while others had flatbed trucks. Some had station wagons, and some had pushing carts.

Some would chant, "Watermelons red to the rind, apples, peaches, and pears—get your fresh fruit right here."

Bells rang while music played as someone else yelled, "Fresh fish, fresh fish." There was another man who was selling fresh chickens, and some were alive.

A man carried a large ice pick, and he would say, "Iceman is here!" Many of the neighbors had iceboxes. When the ice man would open his ice truck, vapors of steam came out of the back of his truck when he opened the door. The steam from the dry ice rushed out into the air like small clouds. Mother would get a piece of dry ice and put in the bathtub, so Cookie could watch the fog fill the bathroom.

Someone else yelled, "Here comes the milkman!" The milkman dressed in all white and drove a white truck to deliver glass bottles of milk to almost every house in the neighborhood.

"Get your mustard, turnips, collard greens, potatoes, and juicy corn on the cob over here!"

Cookie's excited! There's no parade of goodies without the ice cream man; of course, he's there too.

"Come on and get your banana floats, ice cream sundaes, and ice cream cones!"

Her favorite ice cream is the vanilla and chocolate swirl ice cream cone. The ice cream man could be heard through the loudspeaker on top of the ice cream truck as he drove the truck slowly down the street.

Cookie found it hilarious watching the power of persuasion used by women as they negotiated deals for

"COOKIE" A WOUNDED HEALER

food while others used their beauty in an effort to persuade the merchants to reduce prices. All kinds of techniques were used by both the sellers and the customers.

The children laughed and played in the street while others were in line for ice cream. Children compared the height of their ice cream cones to measure which child had the tallest. The seniors sat on their porches watching the excitement, calling out to the merchants to come to them. Some seniors refused to walk, while others were disabled and could not walk.

Ms. Bee, on the other hand, is often overheard gossiping with Mrs. Washington about Ms. Thelma, who lived in the corner house by the alley. "Oh, girl, it's a shame how Thelma flirt with Roger! She knows that's Nancy's brother-in-law's cousin! He married, ain't he?"

Those old ladies were funny, talking about folks, telling half-truths because they didn't know the whole story. The parade of merchants went on for a few hours, and it's the neighborhood's excitement. She never wanted it to end.

"Mommy, someone's at the door," said Cookie. It's the deliveryman; let him in?"

He brought cases of liquor into the living room.

"Girl, come on and help me put these bottles away. Be careful not to break the bottles. Gin goes here, scotch goes over there, and vodka lines up on the left side over there."

"Mommy, where do you want me to put the rum? Mommy, I can put the whiskey over here if you want me to."

She hungered for time and affection from her mother, and if it took helping to place liquor just to spend time with her so be it..

The Good, The Bad, And The Very Ugly

Before they finished stocking the liquor bottles, there's another knock on the door, and it's Uncle Richard, the numbers runner. He came to collect the number of money used to bet on the horse races. She had a lot of uncles and aunts, and it seemed like everyone who came over, Mother introduced them to her as aunts and uncles.

"Cookie, give Uncle Richard my numbers. Richard, box numbers 123 and play numbers 234 straight and put two dollars in each way."

"Okay, yes, Mommy."

Uncle Richard took the papers from her hand, and while saying goodbye, he peeked over his shoulder because he wanted to know what Lia's doing. If bootlegging wasn't illegal enough, being a number runner should be?

The Easter holiday is getting closer, and mother brought two rabbits. "Oh good, I'll play with them, and no one will hurt you," she said to the rabbits. "You, I'll call Bunny and you Bobby." *It's good to have new pet friends after losing Duchess and Twinkles,* Cookie thought.

Mr. Pete, however, stayed on her mind. She thought, *Please, Uncle Pete, don't come over here. I don't want them to hurt you; you are a kind man.* As soon as that thought came, it left and replaced by the Easter holiday.

Easter is only a few days away, and she could hardly wait to wear one of her pretty dresses, white lace socks, and black patent leather shoes and to take her rabbits with her to grandma's house.

Easter finally arrived, "Cookie, get your things; time to go to your grandparents."

"COOKIE" A WOUNDED HEALER

"Wait a minute, Mommy," she said as she called out to Bunny and Bobby. "Mommy, they're not here. Where are they?"

Mother hesitated before responding, Cookie continued looking through the house. *Maybe they're downstairs in the basement*, she thought. Her mother told her the truth: "I cooked them for Easter Sunday dinner. I thought you knew why I bought them."

She shouted, "No! No! No! Mommy! No, they were my friends!"

She went numb. "Mom please can you call the cab I want my grandparents!" Mother and her friends enjoyed baked rabbit smothered in gravy and onions. *Mommy had no reason for allowing the rabbits to be my pets she knew she would cook them for Easter dinner. No rabbit dinner smothered in gravy for me*, Cookie thought.

SECTION THREE:

He's There All the Time

Chapter Eleven

A Fun Day at the Beach

The phone rang.

Grandma said, "Hello, good morning?"

"Mom, it's me. Get Cookie ready because I'm taking her with me today. We're going to the beach, and after we're going fishing, so I will be there shortly, okay? Bye." Lia didn't allow the time for her mother to respond.

After grandma hung up the phone, she laid her hands on her grandbaby and said, "Baby, let's talk to the Lord. Father, thank you for waking us this morning; we give you, thanks and honor for keeping us safe. Please protect us throughout this day and keep us out of harm's way, amen."

Cookie agreed "Amen."

Now get ready because your mother is on her way. *Did grandma pray earlier now she's praying again? I hope everything is okay. It may be nice, my mother and I can have fun, though.*

Mother came, and the car is full of adults but no children. Another car followed, and it too is filled with more people, but no kids, Cookie is the only child.

"COOKIE" A WOUNDED HEALER

Once at the beach, Lia's cousin, Boyce said, "Come on, Cookie. Let's go for a swim!"

Boyce knew she couldn't swim. Her heart was beating hard and fast like the rapid fire of a machine gun; *Oh Lord, I'm scared—I can't catch my breath. He doesn't care. Oh please, don't let him throw me into the water; I can't swim!* Boyce picked her up, threw her over his shoulders, and ran and stood in the water waist deep. Fear gripped her heart, and she was in terror as he began to spin her around like a javelin. All she could see was the water below her. Around and around she went, she screamed as loud as she could, "Help! Somebody help me, please put me down! I can't swim!" She begged for help, her fingernails clawed into his skin. She thought death was imminent. Her mouth wide open, she screamed at the top of her lungs, but no words came out. He ran out of the water and threw her; she landed in the sand. The grown-ups all laughed.

Chapter Twelve

Fish Not Biting

*H*er heart still raced as she lay on the sand whimpering, trying not to cry. Boyce came over to her and said, "Let me help you up. I'm playing. I'm sorry".

She did not allow him to help her. She said, "No, thank you!" so she wiped the sand from her body and walked over to her mother. Lia is engaged in conversation. Cookie waited, hoping her mother would come to her defense by telling Boyce he's wrong. She didn't address the issue and only said, "Come on everybody. Time to go fishing."

Cookie and all of her mother's friends entered into the boat. The radio immediately began playing loud music. Her mother and friends snapped their fingers and clapped their hands and gyrated to the music.

"Hey guys, who have the liquor?" said Boyce, and someone else said, "Don't forget the fishing gear." Boyce, said, while giggling, "Everything and everyone is accounted for including Little Cookie."

The boat passed buoy after buoy and now they were far out in the ocean. The waves were calm, yet

"COOKIE" A WOUNDED HEALER

breathtaking as they moved in concert with the wind as if dancing together. The ocean and the heavens transitioned themselves together with no beginning or end. One flowed into the other as far as the eye could observe it's impossible to separate the two. The sun shone on the waves of the water like the flawlessness of precious stones together they reflected the light of their brilliance. On the horizon, seagulls dived into the water, fishing for food.

She's taken by the beauty and glory of God's creation and all of its awesomeness. It's as though God showed off, like little children wanting attention. The flirting of the wind to the waves as the sun danced on the sea, its light flirted back with multitudes of colors not yet assigned names by man.

Within her heart she ponders on the spectacular view, *Is anyone else on this boat other than me beholding how wonderfully awe-spiring God is? Who's God's counselor, who instructed Him? How did He make everything so beautiful, yet beyond explanation and the comprehension of humans?*

Mother and her friends laughed, danced, and drank alcohol. *Is what they are doing more important than the beauty of God's creation*, thought Cookie?

"Cookie put on your sweater."

"Okay, Mommy."

"Wait a minute. Before you button your sweater, let me attach this line to your button. Now button it up."

Lia put a worm as bait on the end of the hook. "If a fish takes the bait he will pull you overboard to eat you." They all laughed, except Cookie. She's immune to the joke, and she's not smiling. A frown of disgust filled her face. She began to pull the line out of the water little

FISH NOT BITING

by little. Higher and higher, she raised the line from the water, seaweed hung off the hook. Hoping her mother doesn't notice she's disobeying her, all of a sudden, she heard, "Drop the line back into the water!" Her mother's friends burst into laughter. Cookie thought, *what is so funny? I don't want a fish to pull me overboard." Why won't they stop, their laughing is unbearable.* They were all intoxicated however but not only with alcohol, but they were also drunk with carelessness. Careless with their lives as well as the life of a child.

She leaned over on the side of the boat where she's sitting, and said, "Please, fish, wherever you are, please don't eat me." Cookie was thinking, *if I ever needed my grandmother, it is right now.* As she gazed into the water, her reflection stared back as to say, "I see you," so as not to disturb the adults and said to the reflection, "I don't want to die like this."

The boat stopped, and her heart started racing, and her palms began to sweat. She began to look around while saying to herself, *"It's stuck on something, but what it could be? There's nothing out there. In fact, fish weren't biting.* Her heart stopped racing. She took a chance to pull the line from the water. Her mother's attention is not on her because she had a bigger issue at hand: how would they free the boat before it got dark? The sun begins to set. Fear and helplessness shifted from Cookie to the grown-ups. The debate escalated. Lia said, "Who's going to jump out of the boat to find what's causing it to be stuck"? So back and forth they went, like a tennis match. Not one of them wanted to get into the water to find out why. "Boyce, you jump out the boat!" "Lia, you jump!" "No, you jump, I am not going to jump, and you do it!" They became afraid,

"COOKIE" A WOUNDED HEALER

feeling helpless. Someone turned the music off as the debate continued.

Cookie, on the other hand, is happy she wouldn't be eaten by fish. *They're not laughing at me now,* she thought. *In fact, they're not laughing at all.* Suddenly, her eyes met another set of eyes she'd never seen before. It's a man whose skin shone like polished brass like as if he had a tan. On his head, he wore a wide-brimmed brown hat. He had on a lumberjack shirt and deep-sea fishing gear. She couldn't tell if this man is standing in the water, swimming, or floating. He's in the water by the side of the boat where she's sitting. He never spoke to her; however, he kept his eyes fastened on her. Lia and Boyce continued their tennis match of words back and forth while the rest watched. Not paying the man any attention, they continued their debate as to who would get out of the boat. The man lifted the side of the boat where Cookie is sitting and freed it. That's when all the adults noticed him. At that moment he disappeared; he's gone! "You can take the fish line out of the water and unhook it from your sweater," said her mother. Little did Lia know Cookie had taken it out of the water.

Mother said, "I apologize for frightening you." "And so do we," said Lia's friends. "Yeah me too," said Boyce.

They sobered up and were confused at what happened. They all were bewildered. The sense of bewilderment didn't stop there. The boat ride back to the shore was long and mysterious. None of the adults turned the music on. They waited before turning on the boat's engine. All is still and quiet without any human understanding of that man: who is he and how could

FISH NOT BITING

he get there without a boat? The ocean became louder than their thoughts. The sound of the ocean is majestic. It 's methodical as the unisons of the winds carried the waves as they gently pushed the boat. The winds and the wave were in perfect harmony as a sound of an orchestra of harps, cellos, and violins. The waves were the strings while the winds were its fingers playing the strings. The waters gingerly tapped the sides of the boat like the sound of a distant thunder keeping the rhythm of the bass drum. There's absolutely no question it is heaven's symphony. They realized God is the Conductor of the heavenly symphony in total control of them and the vessel. The winds, the waters, all obey Him. Cookie's no longer afraid.

Once at grandma's house, she could hardly wait to tell grandmother about the man who saved her life. *Could the man be an angel?* Cookie thought. Grandma reminded her of the prayer she prayed, asking the Lord to take care of her, and said, "Baby, God is real. The scripture says He watches over all belonging to him. It's almost like a mother hen watching over her baby chicks. He has angels they are sent from heaven to care for us. You will come to realize how faithful God is."

Chapter Thirteen

Drinking and Driving Don't Mix

   nytime Mother said, "Let's go somewhere, "Cookie is suspicious. Off they went on another road trip. Lia always had her friends for company, so Cookie took a friend for the ride too. She played with a stuffed rabbit only (no more real rabbits for friends or dinner).

 Music, drinking, and driving doesn't mix well. She wished she could stay with her grandparents instead of going on a road trip.

 "Don't drive so fast, watch your speed! I think the radar picked up our speed. Slow down! You all hear sirens in the distance? Lia said to the driver, step on it! Lose the police! It's opened liquor in this car"! Cookie looked and sure enough on the backseat floorboard an open bottle of liquor. She remembered her grandmother's prayers, "Lord, take care of little granddaughter and be mindful of her." The music went off as before when they were on the boat. The debate began. "We all are going to jail someone said in a panic. We

DRINKING AND DRIVING DON'T MIX

ain't sold no liquor; we ain't got any money either to pay bails. Yeah, that's right its' a case of liquor in the trunk too"!

"It's too late for regrets," someone else said. We all knew it's illegal to transport alcohol without a liquor license. And above all, we all been drinking."

"Who's going to take care of this child if I get arrested?" said Lia.

Cookie had her rabbit clutched tightly in her arms when she heard an audible voice say, "Unzip the bottom of your bunny rabbit's pouch and put the bottle inside of it." She turned around to spot who spoke to her. She thought, *What a gentle voice. I haven't heard that voice before. Okay, I'll do it.* She turned again to her left and to her right, then to the front seat, listening for the voice. She perceived whoever spoke to her wasn't physically in the car.

The police sirens became louder and louder, and the car slowed because the police were approaching. Lia said, "Just pull over."

"Good afternoon, ma'am, and what bring yawl down here?" Not waiting for an answer, he told them, "I pulled you over because you were speeding. Has anyone been drinking? Any open containers of alcohol in the car? You'd tell me the truth, wouldn't ya?"

"Yes, sir," said Lia. "No alcohol here, sir."

The police officer said, "Yawl, out of the car. Yawl goin' to the police station." Cookie was frightened for all of them.

At the police station, she held her rabbit ever so tight because of the alcohol inside. The officer looked at her, and he took another long look at the rabbit. She knew the officer knew they were lying. A different officer

"COOKIE" A WOUNDED HEALER

appeared from the rear of the station, one she hadn't seen. This police officer is different from the rest of the officers although they were dressed in the same uniforms. His eyes and his smile made him captivating as though he could read a person's entire life. His eyes were piercing like an eagle' eyes and yet divine, as if his eyes spoke, "They are guilty but because of you, a little girl, all are freed." The officer's eyes were still fixed on her. He told the other officers, "Dismiss this case. Let them pay whatever money they have and leave." They were free to leave in their guilty state. This is just like God although our sins are like crimson He makes them white as snow. The mercy of God is everlasting.

"Come on!" said Lia. "Let's get out of this town at once!"

It wasn't long before they questioned themselves about the liquor bottle in the backseat. "Cookie," said one of the men in the car, "did you have the liquor bottle?"

"Yes, I put it in the bottom of my bunny rabbit," she said. She's the star for the rest of the journey.

The liquor stayed inside of the rabbit for the remaining drive back home. The incident with the police changed their minds about the road trip. No longer were they intoxicated—at least, while they were on their way back home. Had it not been for the voice Cookie heard, they all would have gone to jail. Cookie thought *I can't wait to tell grandma this one. I was so afraid for them, I know my grandma would say that's the mercy of God. At times when we are wrong, God covers our guilt and shame. It's His mercy and His grace because He loves us so.*

Chapter Fourteen

An Unattended Child Is A No!

*T*he telephone rang. "Hey, Lia, let's go to the club tonight."

"I don't think I can," she said, "because I don't have a sitter for Cookie."

Lia remembered how her dad scolded her for being so irresponsible. However, it didn't take much prompting; Lia changed her mind and decided to go. *I'll go for a little while Cookie can stay in the car. She'll be fine I won't stay long,* she thought. "Bee I'll come but I definitely cannot stay more than an hour, okay?' Bee replied, "Okay bye." In the car and off they went. Cookie, thought, *well children aren't allowed in bars, so mother must be driving me to grandmas and besides, I have on my pajamas. This is not the way to grandma's house; she lives in the other direction.* "Mother, where are we going to? Grandma's house is the other way"? She never responded.

They pulled into a parking lot of the neighborhood bar, and she got out of the car and said, "Stay low in the backseat, and I'll be right back."

"COOKIE" A WOUNDED HEALER

It's dark, and she's afraid, hoping no one would notice her in a car alone. She laid on the floorboard of the backseat. She heard cars pulling up on the graveled parking lot and people talking as they were exiting their cars and others as they walked by.

"Mommy is taking too long. She has forgotten me out here," she said aloud to herself. The car windows began to fog rapidly—they fogged like curtains being drawn to hide her. She hoped no one saw her in the car. Plus, it's cold and she's afraid. The night began to deepen, darker and colder and quieter it became—one hour, two hours, and two and half hours passed and still no mother.

Please, mommy, come to get me, she thought; as she tried to wedge herself under the seat so people could not catch sight of her. If they saw inside they would've known she was inside afraid and cold. She heard a man's voice, and it sounded like it's getting closer. She heard a woman's voice too.

"You actually had a child in this car all the time? You're kidding me!"

The car door opened. "Seriously, you didn't leave a child in the car!" The man looked around in the car. He squinted, trying to focus on the inside of the car. A look of confusion and bewilderment filled his face.

"Where is she? I don't see her," said the man. All of a sudden, a little girl rose out of the darkness. "Bring this child inside! It's cold out here!" Cookie saw him before he saw her. He took her inside and all eyes were on her.

Cookie to notice to the man's eyes they are familiar— like the ones on the man by the boat and the officer at the police station. The people in the bar all took notice of the tiny little person. They gave her a lot of attention

AN UNATTENDED CHILD IS A NO!

by talking and caring for her. Lia's uncomfortable and ready to leave. She's confronted by shame as she overheard someone say, "What a bright-eyed little girl and she is so small and young too? Did she leave her alone in a car? It's a shame, and her mother is less than a mother. Her Mother should be ashamed of herself and locked up in jail." Cookie felt loved by those people, unlike Lia's other friends. She wasn't laughed at nor was she the brunt of a joke.

They left the neighborhood bar. Mother was certainly quiet the entire ride back home.

Chapter Fifteen

Look Both Ways

  Cookie called her grandparents that morning and told them what her mother did. Lia's parents scolded her for leaving her all alone in a car. Not to mention having a child at a bar. Grandpa said, "Cookie, give Lia the telephone. "Lia, how irresponsible you don't get it? You are so selfish and you ought to be ashamed of yourself! Hold on I'm putting your mother on the phone". Lia said nothing at all. She held the phone away from her ear and stared at Cookie for telling. Not long after the incident, Lia and Cookie went to her parents' home, and Lia decided to stay to spend the day with them. Grandma needed some items from the store so Lia wanted to send Cookie to the store by herself, despite her mother's protest. Before Cookie left, grandma kneeled down to eye level with her, making sure she understood having her repeat every instruction to the letter. "Make sure you look both ways before crossing the street. Make sure the light is green and the sign says walk, ok?"

  She nodded her head yes. Grandma knew why she told her to repeat the instructions. However, Lia wanted

LOOK BOTH WAYS

to prove to her mother just how much she's babying her. Now she's in the middle of their tug of war. "Mom, you're worrying too much. Cookie, go to the store now" said, Lia.

Cookie thought, *this is easy, red light means stop, and a green light means go; that's easy. Okay, one stick of butter and one loaf of bread and some candy,* She keep repeating grandma's instructions and the list of items to buy so she wouldn't forget. W*alking to the store is not such a bad idea. Oh boy, I'm glad this lady came I will cross the street with her.* They both were at the street corner waiting for the light to turn green to walk across. The lady crossed the street before the light turned green. Cookie lost her new found confidence. The street is wider and longer than she thought. This is the very first time she walked anywhere alone. She said to herself, *wow this is a lot different than riding in a car. So much to look out for. Cars are moving fast and people are everywhere and everything so fast-paced.*

The light turned green, time to walk, she looked to the right, left, and right again and stepped off the curb. "Okay, you can do this". Before she reached the other side, she saw the bus coming so fast, *he's not going to stop he's going to hit me what should I do,* she thought. At that point she froze, not wanting to feel the impact and closed her eyes tight as she could. Just before the point of impact, something or someone picked her up and placed her on the opposite side of the street corner. When she opened her eyes she was right where she started from. Cookie started thanking God in her heart, *thank You, Lord, for answering all of grandma's prayers. She knew something would happen to me thank You! I'm not going back across the street*

59

"COOKIE" A WOUNDED HEALER

ever. She turned and ran back to the house. "Mommy and grandma, guess what happened to me?" Where's the stuff I told you to get? Did you come back here empty-handed? Says, Lia. Cookie begins to tell her story trying to regain her composure but she couldn't stop trembling and talking fast. " I never made it to the store as I started crossing the street a bus almost hit me and when I opened my eyes I was back on this side of the street so I ran home". What! What did you say? "I never made it to the store I started crossing the street a bus almost hit me and when I opened my eyes I was back on this side of the street so I ran home! You make no sense at all, Lia's furious. Grandmother, on the other hand, praised God when she heard the story and said, "Thank You Lord for Your divine heavenly hosts, the angels they do what You say. Lia baby, the scriptures say the angels of the Lord are encamped around those who fear Him. He watches over His word to bring it to past. This is why I am praising Him for keeping her safe. Don't be upset my daughter because you don't understand". "Mom, I'm going home, I've had enough! You can stay Cookie and I will pick you up tomorrow. If not I'll call a taxi for you". Grandma kissed Lia on the cheek and said: "drive safe and call me when you get home". After she left, Cookie she ran over to where her grandmother sat and dropped to her knees, laid her head in her grandmother's lap. She began to tell her the story again. Amidst all of the excitement, she forgot to ask her mother about the 4th of July. "Grandma tomorrow is the 4th of July I'm so happy I did not die. I hope my mom is not too angry with me so we can watch the fireworks together." Cookie raised her head, waiting for a response. Grandma nodded and Cookie laid her head

LOOK BOTH WAYS

back down on grandma's lap. Grandma begins to hum her favorite song and she rubbed Cookie's head to comfort and quiet her.

Chapter Sixteen

House of Pestilence

*I*t's the Fourth of July, 1971. At nightfall, the skies welcomed fireworks shows since they are a part of our nation's fabric. Missiles of fire art with the multiple effects and explosions barrage the skies. The sound of the gunpowder as it exits the canons the explosions could be felt throughout the body. The bigger the fireworks display, the louder the boom, the louder the applause.

Cookie loved the Fourth of July. *Oh, how much fun to witness the sky arrayed in such splendor*, she thought.

"Mother, are we going to a cookout on the National Mall and watch the fireworks?" *I can hardly wait I hope she says yes? I'm glad it's on Sunday our house is usually quiet; no parties. Hopefully, she says yes then we can go,* Cookie thought.

While thinking of July Fourth, her mother told her, "I thought this year we'd go over to Aunt Bee's to celebrate. I've brought you some fireworks, and some of my friends' kids will be there, it will be fun". What a loud disappointment. It sounded like 3 firecrackers going off in Cookie's heart. Oh, the thought of it all,

HOUSE OF PESTILENCE

to be with mother at the card party with fireworks at a house infested with bugs—chinches, they called them— the disappointment exploding like a bomb in her heart. Mother and her friends laughed and made jokes about those nasty bugs. Aunt Bee didn't mind the jokes she laughed too. Chinches crawled on tables on the floor and on the walls, bugs marched through the house like little soldiers. Cookie hated being there and hated being bitten by the nasty little critters. The bugs came out at night, and if she'd sit in the chair or lay on the bed, they would bite. She'd step on them or swat bugs off of her clothes. Cookie thought *I'm afraid to sit down, stand up, or to sleep at Aunt Bee's house because of these blood-sucking menaces. I don't know why she wants me to call her my aunt, she's not my aunt she's nasty. I rather go home than to stay here. I hate it! I don't want anything here at all. Oh man, there's a bug right there climbing on the cake! I'm itchy all over. I'm missing the fireworks I want to leave now!*

Something extraordinary happened to mark the end of an era. Cookie's on guard, waiting for the onslaught of the bedbugs, when all of a sudden, the bugs avoided crawling on her. Something or someone had created a barrier between her and them. The bugs began to turn away as if they had been being sprayed with an invisible supernatural bug repellent. She didn't receive one bug bite the entire night!

SECTION FOUR:

Year of Demarcation

Chapter Seventeen

Uninvited Guests

Some unwelcomed guests show up at her grandparents' home. Three of them came and her grandparents' wanted them to leave immediately. Although they wanted them to leave her grandparents were powerless to demand these intruders to leave.

It's getting late and time to go to bed. "Give your grandpa a hug and kiss goodnight," said grandma. "Good night grandpa. Cookie and her grandmother walked down the hall to grandma's bedroom. They prayed and after prayer, they climbed up into grandma's bed with the help of a step-stool.

Usually, Cookie awakened by the smell of fresh bread baking, but this time, no smell of fresh bread or breakfast cooking to tickle nose down to her belly.

In her grandparents' living room stood what appeared like three men and each appeared oddly different. The first, quite tall in stature and his appearance likened the smoke of a burning candle wick. His eyes, dark, piercing and set back in his head. He smells like musty socks.

"COOKIE" A WOUNDED HEALER

The second appeared in the silhouette of a man. He's the blackest black blacker than a thousand midnights. He's absent of any light and enveloped in total darkness. If anyone gets close to him the very life would be sucked out of the person. The third is more hideous than the others. He has no color as if he were transparent. He's dumpy in stature with many arms. His arms are like tentacles of an octopus and he reeks of the scent of rotten fish.

She asked each of them without opening her mouth, "Who are you and why are you here? She waited absent of any fear for an answer. The first one, without opening his mouth, responded. The second responded without opening his mouth as did the third. These beings were dreadful to look upon They responded in succession, "My name is Cancer," as he stepped backward to set in grandma's chair. "My name is Disease" whilst he stood on the left of grandma's chair. "And, my name is Death" he appeared to hover by the back of her chair. Cookie stood in total amazement she watched these intruders take their stance. She closed both eyes and rubbed them hoping when she opened them those being would be gone. When she opened her eyes, they were gone! She thought *this is a dream this cannot be happening! I won't tell my grandparents what I saw. I won't let them get my grandma, I won't!*

Things began to change at her grandparents' home. Grandma began to talk about going away someday. Cookie called on one of her friends, Mr. Time, and asked him to stay because of what her grandmother had said. Grandma's prayers shifted from the usual prayers of asking to demand God. She said, "Lord You are so good to me and You answered every one of my prayers

UNINVITED GUESTS

and I need You to take over right now. Lord, take full responsibility for my grandbaby. I have no one else but You. Amen."

Cookie sensed something shifted in the atmosphere, but what, she couldn't tell until later. The next morning, Cookie was in the living room with her grandpa neither one was talking. Grandpa started cooking more, and sometimes he would turn on the radio and play worship music. Cancer became uncomfortable. Although Cancer hated hearing praises about God, he would not leave, and his silence is so loud.

Grandpa sat quietly in his chair, noticeably quieter than usual. A man of few words, somewhat like Twinkles, but he kept his eyes fixed on grandma's chair. Cookie watched her grandpa and thought, *could he see the man sitting in grandma's chair? I wonder if he can see the others? If I were bigger I'd put Cancer out!*

Other entities appeared in the room and stood erect by the four walls of the entire room. They wore golden sashes across their breast and their names illuminated like a heartbeat across the front of the sash. These beings stood shoulder to shoulder around the walls of the living room. On the far right side of bay living room window, stood, Peace. Next to him stood Power. On the opposite wall, stood, Healing. The last one is named Authority. His name shone the brightest of all flickers of gold and beryl illuminated his name more than the rest. Cookie's in awe and wondered, *can granddaddy see these? I've got to be dreaming? Why are they here? Why wouldn't they help to put Cancer out of grandma's chair?* While she thought on these things, Mr. Time appeared and said, "They needed instruction from her grandparents. *If only her grandparents believed they*

69

"COOKIE" A WOUNDED HEALER

could do something about what you see. The injustice of sickness, disease, and death— it's not impossible for some to assume they are powerless over the three, sickness, disease, and death. Once a human comes into the knowledge of the Kingdom of Heaven and it's Christ God grants power over these three. Some fail to realize that the Kingdom of Heaven is more than meat and drink. It's the will of God with on. One day you will understand".

"I'll dress the big chair in my bedroom, the one by the window, for a bed for you to sleep on," said grandma.

"Can I sleep with you?"

Grandma knew if she died in her sleep while Cookie lay next to her, it would be devastating for her. The next morning, she awoke, looking for grandma from her bed-like chair. Her bright eyes peered out from under the blanket as she waited for a response. With anticipation, she cried out with a loud voice, "Grandma!"

The world could come to an end by an atomic bomb or another flood over the earth. Nothing else mattered, so long as grandma is in the world with her. Again, she peered from under the blanket to check if her grandmother is awake. She's not there. *Where could grandma be?* She's not there. Her heart pounded in her chest so loud, one could hear her blood rushing like water over a stream. She jumped out of the chair, ran down the long hallway, and with each step, her mind flashed like a flash bulb from a Kodak camera. Cookie's mind opened like a photo book of her memories. Memories of her rabbits Bunny and Bobby, Twinkles the cat with his long whiskers, and Duchess her dog, the silky black retriever, and those yellow canaries who made such sweet melodies.

UNINVITED GUESTS

She drew closer to the living room, all she heard was sobbing, and the sobbing grew louder with each step she took. There sat grandma, and as she lifted her head and locked eyes with Cookies. She followed her grandmother's eyes as she slightly tilted her head toward her hands. Her eyes are fixed watching every one of her grandmother's movements. *What's grandma staring at in her loving hands—hands picked cotton and cleaned for other's hands paid to put her daughter through graduate school.* Those same hands held a little girl safe from a cruel world, and there lay, in those same hands, her dying bird.

Oh, how her heart bled for her grandmother. She thought *grandma's loving hands soothed all fears caressing the little lifeless body of her bird of the last canary she has. Oh, my friend Mr. Time, why do you come and not stay? Stay a little while longer, please?* As she stood watching the little bird transition from life to death, she thought, *Birdie, please wake up. How am I to console the only one who consoles me? Grandma loves you, Birdie, and this awful and dreadful cancer is here. Please don't leave grandma.*

The house grew quieter and quieter. No more singing no more smell of bread baking; Grandpa's not whistling like before, he sat in his chair staring into space. Go away, Cancer! You are trying to deafen us.

Chapter Eighteen

An Appointment to Keep

*T*his particular night, like no other grandma, brushed Cookie's hair, she didn't talk much as before. Grandma spoke with the Lord and Cookie overheard their conversation Grandma continued talking to the Lord, her voice became a little louder. *I shouldn't listen I feel like I'm eavesdropping,* thought Cookie. Apparently, grandma wanted her to listen. She asked the Lord, "If you don't mind, will you keep a watch over her? Lord, please be mindful of my granddaughter." She asked without any reservation, "Lord, please remember me. Lord You know she needs protection from this cruel world, Amen."

"Come on and let me tuck you into the chair, I want to make sure you're tucked in because it's a little cool tonight". Grandma reached down and kissed her on the cheek, and said: "Good-bye my sweet little darling." Cookie's bewildered by what grandma said. *Of course, she meant good night; right? She made a mistake.* "Goodnight grandma I love you", grandma told her. "I love you too sweetie," grandma said.

AN APPOINTMENT TO KEEP

Cookie awakened by a bright white light piercing through the window so she thought. The light not shining through the window, but instead, this light is in the room. More startling is the light is alive; it appeared to pulsate. She glanced over the left arm of the chair to look at her grandmother, she thought, *this is a dream.* There, in the light, an image so engulfed by the light, it appeared like a man with his arms folded. He's brilliant, with a golden girdle around his waist. She felt an overwhelming sense of protection in the grandmother's bedroom an overwhelming feeling of peace, love, security, and joy, all wrapped up in this being, so she slept.

The summer break had ended. School's back in session. A call came over the classroom's intercom: "Please send Cookie to the principal's office." The kids in the classroom made fun of her, saying she's in trouble, of course, but she paid the kids no attention. She's too busy thinking about what it could be. She thought as she walked to the principal's office, *Can't be the rabbits, can't be the birds, no, and it cannot be? Oh God, I hope it's not! no no, please!*.

The principal, said, "Your mother called and said to come home right away."

"Yes, ma'am." She rushed out of the school doors, but the faster she walked, it seemed the slower she was moving and the longer it would take, so she began to run fast as she could because fear gripped her being.

She arrived at her grandparents'. Her school is closer to her grandparent's home. After she opened the door, she focused her attention directly on grandma's chair, and it empty. Cancer's gone? She assumed all three were gone. She's so excited because the chair is empty. To her surprise, someone else is in the house whom she'd never met before.

"Sir, who are you?"

"My name is Grave."

Confused she walked away, leaving him, to find someone who she knew.

"Where is everyone?" she said aloud. "Why is he here? and why is his name Grave?" Mr. Time appeared and said, "Child, he came to take your grandmother's body away."

She ignored him she and rushed by him to get to her grandmother's room. She called out to her grandmother as loud as she could. Neighbors heard the sound of anguish bellowing from her soul she called out to her grandmother with no answer. Her eyes filled with tears as she tried to wipe them away. It's like riding in a car during a terrible rainstorm. As the rain hit the windshield, it's impossible to focus. She tried to look through the tears to fasten them onto her beloved grandmother. Fast as she wiped the tears, the faster the tears would fall. She became like the little bird laid helplessly in her grandmother's hands. Her grandmother is the love of her life and her reason for living, so she continued to cry uncontrollably.

1972 became the year of demarcation. How could a young girl handle the news? This is not twin rabbits or Twinkles' the cat, or Duchess the dog whom the policeman shot in front of her and gave her the bullet casing as a souvenir. The "little" in Cookie died that day! She grew beyond her young years. Her grandmother has died.

Grandmother had a wake in two states. Mother shipped her body home to South Carolina for her final

AN APPOINTMENT TO KEEP

burial. The pain she felt immeasurable. Mr. Time, who she longed to be one of her closest friends, now sat in the limousine, waiting. She said to him, "So now you want to hang around when I've begged you to stay. Well, you can leave now".

Mr. Time didn't leave. Cookie wouldn't get out of the limousine to say a final goodbye. She tried to make sense out of what didn't make sense. The limousine door opened, "My mother, she's gone!" Her face filled with deep pain and guilt. She was once known as the strongest, most courageous woman in the universe now she stood there helpless. It's Lia, Cookie's mother. Lia said, "I'm selfish not considering my mother and my father. I've taken both of my parents for granted. I should've spent more time with them, like you. I want my mother back"!

All of a sudden, her eyes changed from pain and guilt to anger and rage. Not sensing any danger, Cookie wanted so much for them to embrace and console each other. They both were hurting. Both had something in common: grief. She reached to embrace her mother, the only woman she knew. Cookie felt something sharp pressing into her side. It's a switch-blade.

Lia screamed saying, "You! Killed my mother! It's your fault she's dead!"

It's been said the eyes are the windows to the soul, and if must be true because Lia's eyes told the story, her soul's overwhelmed by guilt.

"You killed my mother."

"Mommy, please don't hurt me. I didn't kill my grandmother."

That moment, Time stood still, not because she wanted him to, but because she needed him to.

75

"COOKIE" A WOUNDED HEALER

Who am I and where did I come from? She thought. *Am I related to cancer or is death associated with me? I didn't give them permission, and I never knew them. Why does my mother want to to take my life? Why does she hate me so?* Cookie tried to reason within herself.

Mr. Time helped her to dispel what her mother said and did. Mr. Time said, "Cancer was uninvited. He should've been allowed to come to set in your grandmother's chair. He came to live inside of her to take her to his friend Death. Your mother, Lia, is hurting, and she doesn't know how to handle herself. You're not bleeding; the blade did not cut through your clothing. I didn't allow it. Your life, little girl, is spare. You aren't who she says you are those are lies. Sometimes when people are hurting, such as your mother, hurtful words are spoken that can last a lifetime. Bitterness will fill your heart but you will come to understand that forgiveness will wipe it all away.

With tears running down her face, Cookie told him, "I don't know them. I hate them, cancer and all the rest of those wicked beings. My grandma's gone, and my mother hates me."

So much ran through her young mind, and the only dominant factor stood still in her mind: she feels all alone. Mr. Time said, "Weeping may endure for a night and trouble doesn't last always joy will come."

Chapter Nineteen

Run, Cookie, Run

The only woman she knew who loved her giving her a pet name has left. Life as she knew it is over. As dirt covered grandma's casket; dirt covered her too—the dirt of accusations and shame. She wanted to stay with her granddaddy to help him because was alone. His wife of more than sixty years is gone. Lia didn't take care of her dad as she should. She wouldn't let Cookie stay with him being resentful. Therefore, granddaddy left all alone. Cookie's afraid to stay at home with her mother. She too felt alone and confused. Where could she go? She felt hopeless and helpless.

At twelve years old, how's she to handle to the death of her grandmother? The pain unbearable, she began to run, both literally and figuratively. She did so for years to come. Cookie was so confused and distraught after the funeral. So she decided to take her life into her own hands. She left her mother's home and living on the streets. Many days she ate out of trash cans and slept on park benches and concrete slabs. Sometimes she slept on apartment stairwells. Rodents played in the streets;

"COOKIE" A WOUNDED HEALER

hobos, bums, pimps, dope dealers, prostitutes, robbers, murderers, drunks, drug addicts—could these be her new friends? She's quite familiar with some of these behaviors, and personalities. Some of these people were like those who showed up at her house on the weekends. The streets were dangerous, but the street people protected her from the pimps, drug dealers, and child molesters.

After weeks of living in the streets of Washington, DC, she grew tired and weary and decided to go home. Although the home was tough, it was better than living on the streets. Cookie knocked on the door; it opened, cigarette smoke billowed out, and the stench of alcohol was all too familiar. She heard the sound of the playing cards slapping the table. As she walked by she saw the men rolling the dice over in the corner on the floor. How familiar the sound of laughter when someone won the crap table. In the midst of all of this was the smell of chicken frying. She thought *I'm so hungry; if no more than to eat a piece of hot fried chicken, it's worth the fight to breathe and to put up with mother's friends. My Mother doesn't look so well; she's not complaining? She's not asking me where I've been?*

Mother said to her with no questions asked, "Go in the kitchen, fix yourself a plate of food, and go upstairs to your room".

"Gladly, what a relief,", she said, way down deep under her breath.

Mother asked, " did you say something?" and of course, she answered no because she 's no fool.

All she ever wanted is the love of her mother. Up to her bedroom, she went, and after she finished eating, off to sleep in her own bed.

RUN, COOKIE, RUN

Later in the night, she needed to go to the restroom, but the door wouldn't open. "Mother help me! I can't get out! The door won't open? I need to use the bathroom, please." *Did they lock me in here?* She pulled on the doorknob over and over again. Cookie's mind began to race; thoughts ran into one another. *What's going on?* She could barely hold on to keep from urinating on herself.

All of a sudden, she had a flashback of her mother's strange way of disciplining. Due to all the chaos in their home Cookie never wanted to be there. As a young girl, she became rambunctious. One particular evening, Lia called one of her policeman friends to the house. Cookie thought *I wonder why he's here?*

"Come outside, young lady. You too, Lia," said the police officer. He told them to sit in his police car. The policeman began to question Cookie. The questions came so fast, like rapid fire from an automatic weapon. He interrogated her as if she was involved in a criminal offense. She couldn't think to answer. The officer's questions were mixed with scolding her. "What's your problem? Why won't you obey? Why don't you want to stay home? Why do you want to always go over your grandparents' house? Young lady, do you want to go to jail for hard-headed children? You're a bad girl." Her head hung down, trying to process the reason for his line of questioning.

She began to raise her head in an attempt to answer his questions as best she could. All she thought about was, *I want my grandparents. He's so mean! He's asking me too many questions. I can't think that fast! What do I do now? I can't think. If only he knew what goes on in my house.*

"COOKIE" A WOUNDED HEALER

"Ouch!" she shouted because a knife pressed into her side. Immediately, the flashback of the officer's nastiness left as quick as it came. Cookie looked at her mother with her eyes and mouth wide open in total disbelief.

"Shut up, don't say anything," said her mother. Fear gripped her with no way of escape. She mustered up enough strength with the help of one of her friends, Courage.

She said, "Mr. Policeman, sir, my mother has a knife pressing in on my side, and she is going to kill me."

The officer stared into his rearview mirror with a look of surprise. All interrogation ceased. His demeanor changed, and a puzzling look came over his face. His eyebrows began to rise like he wanted to ask a question but afraid of the answer. The officer thought, *if Lia cuts her I'm ruined?* Cookie continued to look into his eyes through his rearview mirror. He went from being a giant monster in a blue policeman uniform to a small boy in a police uniform. Whatever Lia's intention, he wanted no part of it. The officer said, "Get out my car go back inside with your mother and never say you want to run away again!"

She snapped out of the flashback by needing to relieve herself, so she screamed out, "I've got to go to the bathroom! Come and open the door!" I know you hear me?"

She knew the neighbors probably heard but unable to help. She's almost sure her mother had the police on her payroll. They never came to stop all of the loud music and gambling.

"Go look on your back porch. There's a pot for you to use," female yells. Cookie's afraid, and not sure who

RUN, COOKIE, RUN

the woman is or what she's capable of doing. *I hope my mother and her friend not plotting to hurt me.* She knew how dangerous her mother could be—how they made jokes and laughed after having hurt people. So without asking who's telling her to use a pot to urinate in? Cookie yelled, "I've got to get out of here". Her bedroom has a screened-in back porch, so she cut the screen with scissors tied the bed sheets together and climbed out of the second-floor window.

Running fast as she could down the dark alley into dangerous streets wondering if her mother ever loved her. As she ran she passed a telephone booth and decided to go back to the phone booth to call the only father she knew. *I've never noticed this telephone booth here before?* she thought. *I'm going to call him. What am I going to do if he says no? I sure hope he answers the phone.* She dials the zero for the operator, "hello operator please ma'am this is a collect call from Cookie." "Hello," says the voice on the other end. "Hello again pausing waiting for her to say something, "Cookie! What's wrong are you okay? You're calling me from a pay phone it's 3 am in the morning, says her dad." She's holding the receiver afraid to ask thinking he may say no. Finally, she says, "daddy? He responds, "Yes." She begins to cry uncontrollably and asked, "daddy please I can't take it any longer please may I come home to Michigan with you, and he said, "yes". "The first thing is to make sure you're safe. I need you to go to Ms. Thelma's. I'm going to call her so you stay put I will call right back. Uncle Prince will pick you in the morning and I will call your mom. Don't worry". The very next morning Cookie was on an airplane on her way to Michigan to be with her dad.

"COOKIE" A WOUNDED HEALER

Three years later, in 1975, the telephone rang. "Hello?"

"Jay, may I speak to Cookie? I'm sick and I need her to come home." *Lia's famous at crying wolf,* he thought.

"Cookie," dad says, "Telephone. It's your mother."

She came on the telephone. "Hello?"

"I need you to come home. I'm not well, and I've lost my sight."

Her mother's not alone; she has a new boyfriend, and he has children to help her around the house. Cookie thought, *she never needed her before, Its' hard to believe my mother's blind? I've never been the object of mother's affection, only a child trophy. Perhaps she's not my real mother. Why does she do the things she does?* She sighed, took Courage and told her mother exactly what's on her heart. "Mom, I love you but I am afraid of you. I'm afraid you may put me in a home for wayward youth. You said I killed grandma. I would never hurt anyone. I'm in school doing well ask daddy he'll tell you?

While they spoke, her mother began talking to someone else who apparently walked into the house she said to the person, "It's snowing outside; there's snow on your coat."

Cookie thought, *how could she know if it's snowing if she's blind?* Mother, I'm sorry. I love you, but I'm staying here with Daddy. I don't want you to hurt me anymore."

She waited for her mother to respond but she didn't. "Mother, did you hear me? I'm afraid you may send me to a home for runaway children. I know how you say things not true. If you're blind, how do you know it's

RUN, COOKIE, RUN

snowing, and who are you speaking to? Hello, Mother, hello are you still there?"

"Yes, I'm still on the phone. I'm not going to send you away. I need you, and the person in the background is my friend's son. His name is David, I can see a little. Will you come home, please?" she asked again.

After a long pause, she said, "Mother, I don't know I love you, mom I will think about it and call you back. Cookie did not go back; she remained in Michigan.

Michigan's harsh winter is breaking, giving way to the entrance of March. As March ushers in spring, the phone rang, daddy delayed answering because he's engulfed in his television sports program. "Hello?" His smile gave way to a frown. "Oh God," he sighed. "Okay, I'll tell her. When is it going to be, and where is it going to be?" Daddy slowly put the phone from his ear and walked away.

What had taken his attention? Could something be wrong with my mother? She tried before to trick me into coming home. It's not beneficial crying wolf; it comes a time when something can truly be wrong. Although she wanted to be home with her mother, she's terribly afraid she'd be committed to a home for wayward youth. She yearned for her, but at what expense? Would she again put another knife to her side and this time kill her?

She walked over to her father, he didn't hand her the phone. He stooped down to look at her at her level and said, "Your mother has died."

EPILOGUE

The curtains are pulled back, it is evident a supernatural battle is going on for the soul of this child. She did not enlist herself into this war, as a result of the pain and horror her young life endures, she achieved an overwhelming ability to love. The enemy for her soul meant evil but God turned it around for her good. Through many afflictions, trials, and tests, an invisible God is made visible through supernatural manifestation.

Cookie comes to realize God is a prayer-answering God, and He watches over His Word to perform it. He assigns angelic beings to watch over those whom He loves, and when God says He will never leave you alone, He means what He says. God shows Himself strong and He becomes Lord of her life.

She continued on her journey, a greater manifestation of evil contending for her soul. When the enemy thought the vehicle of evil personalities human agents of the devil inhabited by some individuals failed. The enemy released witchcraft upon her young life. Although the enemy's plan manifested itself in full throttle, God's ultimate plan superimposed the plans of the enemy in turning her pain into purpose.

ABOUT THE AUTHOR

A. J. Hatcher's desire is to live a life which exemplifies the true nature and character of a redeemed life where God Himself gets all the glory, honor, and praise.

For booking engagements or prayer request you can contact the author via email: awounderhealerministries@gmail.com

Printed in the USA
CPSIA information can be obtained
at www.ICGtesting.com
LVHW051257271023
762202LV00021B/1631